STREET CORNER DAD

STREET CORNER DAD

Alan Gibbons

With illustrations by
Ismael Pinteno

Barrington Stoke

To Maisie Long, for the loan of her life

First published in 2015 in Great Britain by
Barrington Stoke Ltd
18 Walker Street, Edinburgh, EH3 7LP

www.barringtonstoke.co.uk

This story first appeared in a different form in
My Dad's a Punk (Kingfisher, 2006)

Text © 2006 Alan Gibbons
Illustrations © 2015 Ismael Pinteno

A CIP catalogue record for this book is available
from the British Library upon request

ISBN: 978-1-78112-437-6

Printed in China by Leo

Contents

Chapter 1
Iron

It never crossed my mind that we would ever be apart. Even when the bombs started to fall on Liverpool, I didn't think they would change anything for my family.

I was born in 1930 and I was nine when the war started. I lived with my family in Bond Street, just off Scotland Road. There were five of us and we lived in a flat with three bedrooms. We were lucky – the people on the other side of the stair only had two. And we

had a hot-water tap and a bath. All they had
was the cold-water tap.

My nan ran the house with a rod of iron.
Kathleen, her name was, and everybody was in
fear of her. She had a face like a hawk and a
taste for Guinness.

Nan had the good bedroom and Mam and Dad had the second bedroom. Me and Molly made do with the box room. Molly was five. She was always whining and her nose ran non-stop.

Dad was often away on his ship. He was a seaman, and he was part of the Battle of the Atlantic. Since the start of the war the Nazis had been trying to keep our ships from crossing the sea to bring us the things we needed. Dad's ship protected merchant ships so Britain could get through the dark days of the war.

Nan never liked Dad, with his "rough sailor ways," as she called them. She didn't think he was good enough for my mum – Nan's daughter.

We were happy, though most people today would wonder what we had to be happy about. It was bread and dripping for tea every day and not much in the way of toys for me and

Molly. There were no fitted carpets or central heating, no cars or TVs or phones. Most nights, the air-raid siren would wail through the mist and we would take ourselves off to the shelter in the Swings.

The Swings was a kind of small, tatty park, with a worn lawn, some maypoles, a bandstand and two kinds of shelter. One shelter was dug into the ground and one was above ground and made of brick. One time, an unexploded land mine was found in the Swings. The houses near by had to be cleared for three days, and we all slept in St Martin's Hall.

The funny thing is, we kids took it in our stride. We ran wild, too. The streets and alleys in our bit of the city belonged to us, even when the Germans started to bomb the docks and it wasn't safe to play out or even sleep at home. Lots of the other kids got sent to North Wales, but Nan said we weren't going, in spite of the damage to the buildings and the roads.

"If it happens, it happens," she said. "At least we'll all go together."

That was that. Anything Nan said was gospel – no one could say any different. Mam found it hard to stand up to her. The only time she did was when she married my dad. And Dad loved Mam, so he didn't stand up to Nan either.

And so that's how we ended up sticking it out at home. For months there wasn't even any school. There just weren't enough kids to keep it running. When school did start again, it was in somebody's front room. You went for a morning, but you didn't learn much. Not that me or Molly cared. We just wanted to go about our business. Like I said, we were happy.

Chapter 2
Like a Puppet

Then it happened.

The evening started with Nan laying down the law. "You're not going down to that dance hall tonight," she told Mam and Dad.

"Oh, come on, Kathleen," Dad said. "We just want to enjoy ourselves. I'm away to sea tomorrow."

Nan was always ready to have a go at Dad. "You never know what might happen," she said.

"That's a bit rich, isn't it?" Dad said. "You're the one who didn't want the kids to go to Wales."

Nan scowled and said they were fools.

Dad just grinned and swept Mam out the door. I could hear their laughter fading into the night. That's the last time I saw them together.

The next day, grey-faced men filled the parlour. Nan sat in her chair, her hawk face white and her black eyes on Dad. Dad sat in the corner with his shoulders hunched. It was as if somebody had ripped the life out of him. He was like a puppet with its strings cut.

It was a while before I understood. Mam and Dad had been in the dance hall when a bomb hit. Some people were killed there – but not Mam. She cheated death the first time. They took her to Mill Road Hospital to be treated for a minor head wound. It was a

million-to-one chance that the hospital would
be hit in the same raid, but in war million-
to-one chances happen. Mam died in the
hospital, where they're supposed to make
people better.

Chapter 3
Splinter

Days later, when the pain was still fresh, I was woken by angry voices. One was Dad's. The other belonged to Nan. As I crept to the door, I felt like there was a splinter lodged in my heart. I already knew what this was about, but I hoped against hope I was wrong.

"Get out!" Nan was screaming at my dad. "Go away to sea, and don't ever come sniffing round this door again."

I wanted to cry out. I wanted to tell her he was my dad and she had no right to talk to him that way. But the words stuck in my throat. Instead I watched them, black figures against the morning sun that was shining in the open door.

"You can't keep me away," Dad said. "Jimmy and Molly are mine. They're my kids and I've a right to see them."

That's when Nan said the words I'll never forget.

"You killed my daughter," she said. "I'll raise her kids. You ..." She stabbed a bony finger at the door. "You get on your ship, and I hope you go down with it. Yes, I hope those German U-boats take you to the bottom of the sea."

But Dad wasn't done yet. He saw me behind the door and he shoved past Nan and strode over to me.

"I'm sorry you had to hear that, Jimmy," he said. "I've got to go away, but I'll be back for you, both of you."

His jacket smelled of salt and tobacco. He stroked Molly's hair, and then he looked at

Nan to make sure she wasn't watching. He slipped a piece of paper with writing on it to me.

"Nothing in this world or any other will keep us apart, Jimmy," he said. "You remember that."

I nodded, and then Dad left. I sat with the piece of paper in my hand and stared after him. Then something snapped inside me. I pulled on my trousers and ran for the door. Nan made a grab for me, but I wiggled away from her grasp and shot into the street. With bare feet I ran, on and on until I saw him in the distance, getting on a tram.

"Nothing will keep us apart, Dad," I yelled, in an echo of his own words. "Not in this world or any other."

I saw him turn around. He waved and then he was gone.

Chapter 4
Blood

It was as if we'd lost both parents in the bombing.

Nan wouldn't hear Dad's name in the house. If me or Molly dared say anything about him, she would give us a back-hander and send us off to bed, no matter what the time. But I had the piece of paper from Dad, and that was something Nan knew nothing about.

After a few weeks, Nan told us there were going to be changes. Uncle Eddie's house had been bombed, so he was going to move into Nan's house with his family. There was Aunt Lizzie and their seven children – Lilly, Nelly, Jane, Mary, Ann, John and little Eddie. I knew I was going to get a hiding for it, but I argued with Nan.

"What about my dad?" I said. "What about when he comes home?"

"You dare say that man's name in this house?" she cried. "After what he did."

"Yes, I dare," I shouted back. "He's my dad, and that's that."

But that wasn't that. Nan got hold of the coal shovel and swung it at me until I gave in and ran to bed. Molly stood and snivelled until Nan bawled at her to stop. We both cried ourselves to sleep that night.

But when Molly dropped off at last, I got Dad's note from a hole in the floor and read it again.

Dear Jimmy

I will always come back for you and for Molly. When I'm in port, my mate Peter Kelly will get a message to you. And then you and Molly are to come and meet me on the street corner next to Scotland Road.

From, your dad

The note was still in my hand when I woke up the next day.

Eddie and Lizzie and their children didn't bother us, for all there were a lot of them. For a start, they gave us a whole new crowd to play with. But there was one person we dreaded seeing in the house. Her name was Marlene Grogan. We never knew where she came from or why she showed up, but when they were together, she and Nan acted like the closest friends you could imagine.

Marlene wore a heavy shawl and always had a smile on her face, as if she was stupid. Nan was fond of a glass of Guinness, but Marlene had it flowing in her veins instead of blood. Whenever Marlene showed up, she and Nan would go on a bender and spend the next three or four days rotten drunk. They would be up all hours singing soppy songs and cackling like a pair of witches.

The worst bit was that Marlene would stagger into our room stinking of booze and then she would sleep in Molly's bed. From one end came the stink of ale and from the other a snore that could rattle the ornaments on the mantelpiece.

"Come home, Dad," I would whisper into my pillow before I dropped off to sleep. "Please come home and take us away."

I lost count of the number of times I had to explain to Molly where Dad had gone.

"He's gone away to sea," I told her.

"Why has he?"

"Because he's got to run the lines ..."

"What does that mean?" Molly asked.

"He's trying to bring food to England," I told her. "The Germans are trying to stop him, so they can starve us out and win the war. Don't you know anything?"

"More than you," she sniffed and walked away.

I was fed up of explaining things to Molly. I just wanted Dad to come home so he could tell her himself and shut her up.

Chapter 5
Coconut

My dream came true that Saturday night. I was playing down at the Swings when a tall, wiry man came along.

"My name's Peter Kelly," he said. "Are you John Byrne's boy?"

My heart skipped a beat. "Yes," I said.

"Did your dad tell you to expect me?"

"Yes."

Peter Kelly smiled. "Well, he's home now, son. When's the best time to meet him?"

"Nan will be down the boozer by 8 o'clock," I said. "Tell Dad that me and Molly will be on the street corner at ten past."

Peter Kelly winked. "He'll be glad to see you."

Dad didn't let us down. Molly and me were on the corner at five past eight. Dad was already there.

Molly threw herself into his arms. I waited for my turn.

"Jerry didn't get you then?" I asked. "Jerry" meant the Germans and I thought it made me sound grown-up.

Dad shook his head. "There isn't a U-boat captain on earth who can catch Johnny Byrne." He put his hand inside his raincoat. "Here," he said. "I brought you something."

It looked like a turnip with whiskers.

"What is it?" Molly asked, her eyes wide.

Because of the war, Molly had never seen fruit. I had all but forgotten what it looked like, but I'd never seen anything like this.

"It's a coconut," Dad said. "You drill a hole in it and drink the milk."

"It gives milk," I gasped. "Like a cow?"

Dad laughed. "Not quite," he said. "There's white stuff inside the shell, too – the pulp. You can eat it." He drew us closer. "And when you've finished the inside, you can cut the shell in half and make a sound like horses' hooves."

The coconut tasted amazing, and we loved listening to the sound of horses' hooves. It was almost as loud as the drone of the Heinkel bombers or the thump of the bombs they dropped.

We hid the coconut from Nan, and she never knew that we'd seen Dad. We met him four times before he had to go away again. One day he even took us to his place.

"A pal of mine lets me stay here," he said.

Dad didn't have anywhere else to go. He didn't have any family. When he was little he got sent to a children's home.

"It was a cold, cruel place," he said. "I used to cry myself to sleep. Some poor kids wet the bed, they were that scared and lonely. That's why you have to put up with Kathleen. Just until this war is over and I can get a job on shore."

Even when Dad had gone back to sea, different things kept him in our minds. Lots of kids were coming back from North Wales, and school had started again. Molly took her half of the coconut in to show the class. She had a teacher named Miss Humphries.

"Molly," Miss Humphries asked, "have you got any of the coconut meat left?"

"Yes and you can have it," Molly said. "I just want to keep the shell to make a sound like a horse."

Miss Humphries was delighted. "It's for my little bird, Billy," she said. "He's had nothing like it since the war started."

That made Molly the teacher's pet. She loved Dad even more for that.

Chapter 6
Shillings

The next time Dad came home and met us on our corner, he had something new. I recognised it right away. It was a banana. Molly didn't know what to make of it.

"You eat it," Dad said.

Molly gave it a brief lick and screwed up her face. "I don't like it," she said.

"Not like that," Dad told her. "You've got to unpeel the skin first." He showed her how. "Now try."

This time Molly stuffed it in.

"So, do you like it?" Dad asked.

Molly's eyes were as round as saucers and her cheeks were puffed up.

"It's lovely," she mumbled. It was hard to make the words out because of the mouthful of banana.

Before Dad went back to his ship this time, he gave us money – three shillings each.

"Don't let Kathleen find it," he said. "She'll only drink it away."

"Don't worry," I told him. "We're good at hiding things from Nan."

But I couldn't have been more wrong. When we got home that night, the light was on in the best room. We thought it was Uncle Eddie and Aunt Lizzie. The moment we walked in the door we saw who it really was.

"Nan!"

"Empty your pockets," she ordered.

"Why?"

"Because I say so."

I tried to stand up to her. "We've got nothing," I told her.

"Empty them out, I say."

Molly was starting to whimper.

"Now look what you've done," I said, in the hope I could change the subject.

Nan wasn't having any of it. "Do it," she said.

The moment I emptied my pockets her eyes fell on the six shiny coins.

"You can't have them," Molly cried as Nan reached for them. "He gave them to us."

I saw the hawk look in Nan's eyes. "Who's he?" she asked.

As if she didn't know.

"I said," she insisted. "Who is he?"

"You know who," I cried. "Dad."

"You've been seeing him behind my back?" Nan yelled.

"Yes," I shouted back. "And we'll see him again. You see if we don't."

Nan scooped up the coins. "We'll see about that," she said.

Marlene stayed for the next three nights. Our coins helped pay for the Guinness.

Chapter 7
Torpedo

The next time Peter Kelly came to tell me that Dad was home, Molly and me took more care than before. We followed Nan all the way to the pub before we went to see him.

"Dad!"

Molly squealed with joy the moment she saw him turn the corner. As usual, I waited my turn. We told Dad about the money. His eyes narrowed and his face went dark.

"The war won't last much longer," he said, as if the Prime Minister was a personal friend and he had special information. "Then I'll take you away from her for good."

"The words were barely out of his mouth when we heard a voice we knew.

"I knew you were sneaking around here," Nan said to Dad. "Turning up to hand out your blood money, as if it would make up for what you did."

"I did nothing," Dad said. "It was the bombs that took your daughter, Kathleen. Your daughter and my wife."

That did it.

Nan flew at him, punching him and slapping him on the face. Dad didn't do a thing. He just stood there and took it. Molly screamed and cried and begged Nan to stop.

"Oh, I'll stop," said Nan. "I'll stop when he says he's never coming back." She was panting from all the shouting. "Don't you come near these kids again," she screamed as Dad walked away. "Ever!"

I know why Dad walked away. He had nowhere to take us. Nan had won.

By then the bombing had stopped, but Dad still had to run the lines. No matter what Nan said, we still found ways to see him when he came home. Then one day Peter Kelly came up to me on Titchfield Street.

"I didn't expect my dad back so soon," I said.

I saw Peter Kelly's face change. My insides turned over.

"What's wrong?" I said.

Peter Kelly looked at his feet. "It's the ship, lad," he said. "It's been reported missing. A torpedo got them."

"Oh, no. No!" I waited a beat. "Were there survivors?"

Peter Kelly shook his head. "There's no word, son. I'm sorry."

I stared at Peter Kelly's face and it felt as if the world had ended.

There was only one thing left to say.

"What do I tell Molly?" I asked, and my heart broke.

Chapter 8
Coal Shovel

That night Molly sobbed and sobbed. I wanted to sob with her, but I knew I couldn't. I had to be strong for her. I put my arms around her, for all she was nearly ten by then. I rocked her and told her that it would be all right.

"You heard what Dad told us that time," I said. "There's not a U-boat captain on earth who can catch Johnny Byrne."

Molly looked at me through her tears. "You really think so?" she asked.

My throat was choked with sobs, but I kept up the brave face. "I know it, Moll."

I became aware of Nan watching from the doorway. Even she didn't dare say anything that night.

"Remember what he said?" I told my sister. "Nothing will keep us apart in this world or any other."

Molly fell asleep that night murmuring the words over and over. I didn't have the heart to tell her that I knew Dad's promise was now nothing but a fairy tale.

Weeks went by. I knew there was no hope, but still I imagined the day that Peter Kelly would come looking for me and tell me that Dad was home. Months went by. Soon I stopped believing he was coming back, even in my wildest dreams. But I pretended, for Molly's sake, and to keep up appearances. What's more, I wasn't going to let Nan think she'd won.

"My dad's coming back," I kept telling her. "Even if it's just to spite you."

I was 14 by then, and nothing Nan did could scare me any more. She could scream and shout, she could shake her fist, she could swing the coal shovel, but nothing made any difference. I just stared back and told her I wasn't scared.

One night I won my first real battle with her. I heard her come in the door with Marlene Grogan. I saw the look on Molly's face as Marlene staggered towards her bed. That's when I made up my mind.

"You can stop right there," I said.

Marlene stood and rocked in shock.

"What's going on?" Nan demanded. Her voice was thick with drink.

"He won't let me in my room," Marlene
said.

"It's not your room," I told her. "And it's not your bed. If you want a bed, you can share with her." I pointed at Nan.

"That's a fine way to talk," Nan said. "After I brought you up."

She reached for the coal shovel, but I got there first.

"Want this?" I said. "You can have it if you like." I waved it in front of her nose. "You hit my dad one time," I said. "And he let you because he's a gentleman. But believe me, Nan, I'm not."

Nan stared for a moment and then turned on her heels. "Come on, Marlene," she said.

"Would you have hit her?" Molly asked me.

"Of course not," I said, and I put down the shovel. "I'm like my dad. A gentleman."

Chapter 9
A Man

I was nearly 15 when the war ended.

There were celebrations in front of
St George's Hall. By the time I got there with
Molly and a few friends, there were thousands
of people dancing, cheering, shouting. Some
of the soldiers were on top of the lion statues,
waving their arms.

"Hard to credit it," somebody said.

I turned around. It was Peter Kelly. I hadn't seen him for such a long time. He looked different – greyer and thinner.

"Six years, and now it's over," he said.

He had a grin from ear. I thought it was because he'd been drinking or just because the war was over at last. Then I heard another voice I knew.

"Dad!"

Molly screamed so loud that half the heads in the crowd seemed to turn our way.

"Dad!"

He swung her around and around. I waited my turn. Dad looked me up and down. "It's been a while," he said.

He reached out a hand and we shook. It was his way of saying that I wasn't a boy any

more. I was a man. I already knew that –
because of the way I'd stood up to Nan.

"What happened to you?" I asked.

Dad drew us to one side and told his
tale. He and a handful of other men made
it to shore when that torpedo hit their boat.
They were taken in by Norwegian resistance

fighters and sat out the war in Norway. They spent most of their time in a cave in the mountains. Dad had tried to get a message to us, but he had no way to know if we had got it.

When Dad finished his story, he hugged both of us.

"Does this mean you've come for us?" Molly asked. "We don't have to go back to Nan's?"

Dad nodded. "I've got your things," he said.

"Didn't Nan try to stop you?" we both asked.

Dad winked. "She tried."

"You didn't hurt her?" Molly asked. "She'll take it out on us if you did. You don't know what she's like."

I could see that she was still scared of the hawk woman and her rod of iron.

"Of course not," Dad said. His eyes twinkled. "I'm a gentleman."

Dad said one last thing before we headed for the tram. His voice was thick with feeling.

"I told you nothing could keep us apart."

All three of us finished the sentence.

"In this world or any other."

Our books are tested
for children and young people by
children and young people.

Thanks to everyone who consulted on
a manuscript for their time and effort in
helping us to make our books better
for our readers.

More *4u2read* titles ...

Nadine Dreams of Home

BERNARD ASHLEY

Nadine finds Britain scary. Not scary like soldiers, or the sound of guns. But scary in other ways. If only her father were here. But it's just Nadine, her mother and her little brother now. They have no friends, no English, and no idea if they will ever see Nadine's father again. But then Nadine finds a special picture, and dreams a special dream ...

Deadly Letter

MARY HOFFMAN

Prity wants to play with the other children at school, but it's hard when you're the new girl and you don't know the rules. And it doesn't help when you're saddled with a name that sounds like a joke.

Will Prity ever fit in?

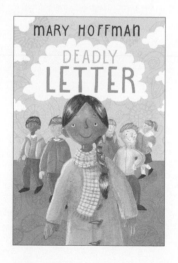

The Hat Trick
TERRY DEARY

A Game of Two Halves ...

Jud's team is 2–0 down in the big match when their goalie is hurt.

Can Jud save the day?

All Sorts to Make a World
JOHN AGARD

Shona's day has been packed with characters.

Now Shona and her dad are on a Tube train that's stuck in a tunnel and everyone is going ... bananas!

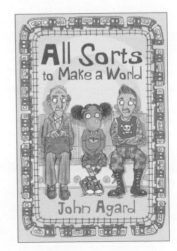

www.barringtonstoke.co.uk

More **4u2read** titles ...

How Brave Is That?
ANNE FINE

Tom's a brave lad. All he's ever wanted to do is work hard at school, pass his exams and join the army. He never gives up, even when terrible triplets turn his life upside down at home. But when disaster strikes on exam day, Tom has to come up with a plan. Fast. And it will be the bravest thing he has ever done!

Gnomes, Gnomes, Gnomes
ANNE FINE

Sam's obsessed. Any time he gets his hands on some clay, he makes gnomes. But Sam doesn't like to have gnomes in his room. So they live out in the shed. But when Sam's mum needs that space, the gnomes will have to go. So Sam plans a send-off that turns into a night the family will never forget!

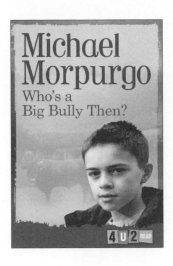

Who's a Big Bully Then?

MICHAEL MORPURGO

Olly is a bull. A very big bull.

Darren Bishop is a bully. A very nasty bully.

What will hapen when one of Darren's victims dares him to take on Olly?

Hostage

MALORIE BLACKMAN

"I'll make sure your dad never sees you again!"

Blindfolded. Alone. Angela has no idea where she is or what will happen next. The only thing she knows is she's been kidnapped. Is she brave enough to escape?

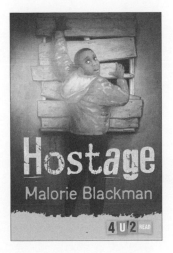